To all those bystanders: Have the courage to help
the torment of others and instead, ask the simple
or say, "That's not right!" To all the victims of
positive, and keep believing in yourself. You
tough times. And you never know; you might j

THE POWER
OF
BYSTANDERS

Willie Bohanon & Friends Learn to
Handle Bullying Like a B.O.S.S.

Written by **KIP "MR. J" JONES**
Illustrated by **CHAD ISELY**

BOYS TOWN
Press®

Boys Town, Nebraska

The Power of Bystanders
Text and Illustrations Copyright © 2015 by Father Flanagan's Boys' Home
978-1-934490-79-2

Published by the Boys Town Press
14100 Crawford St.
Boys Town, NE 68010

For a Boys Town Press catalog, call **1-800-282-6657**
or visit our website: **BoysTownPress.org**.

Publisher's Cataloging-in-Publication Data

Jones, Kip, 1965-

The power of bystanders : Willie Bohanon and friends learn to handle bullying like a B.O.S.S. / written by Kip
"Mr. J" Jones ; illustrated by Chad Isely. -- Boys Town, NE : Boys Town Press, [2015]

    pages ; cm.
    (Urban character education)

    ISBN: 978-1-934490-79-2
    Audience: grades 3-8.
    Summary: This comic book-style children's book shows readers how bystanders can handle bullying like a
B.O.S.S. (Bystanders hold the key; Open your mouth; Stand up for others; Stick together). This is the second
book in the Urban Character Education series.--Publisher.

    1. Bullying--Prevention--Juvenile literature. 2. Bullying in schools-- Prevention--Juvenile literature. 3. Vic-
tims of bullying--Juvenile literature. 4. Interpersonal conflict--Juvenile literature. 5. Bystander effect--Juvenile
literature. 6. Helping behavior--Juvenile literature. 7. Friendship--Juvenile literature. 8. Assertiveness (Psychology)-- Juvenile literature. 9. Children--Life skills guides--Juvenile literature. 10. Adolescents--Life skills
guides--Juvenile literature. 11. [Bullying-- Prevention. 12. Bullying in schools--Prevention. 13. Interpersonal
conflict. 14. Helping behavior. 15. Friendship. 16. Assertiveness (Psychology) 17. Problem solving. 18. Conduct
of life.] I. Isely, Chad. II. Title.

BF637.B85 J66 2015

302.34/3--dc23   1504

Printed in the United States
10 9 8 7 6 5 4 3 2 1

Boys Town Press is the publishing division of Boys Town,
a national organization serving children and families.

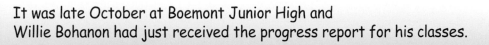

It was late October at Boemont Junior High and
Willie Bohanon had just received the progress report for his classes.

REPORT CARD

MATH _____ A-
ENGLISH _____ A
HISTORY _____ A+
SCIENCE _____ A+
HOMEROOM _____ A
P.E. _____ A+

He had all A's and in the county championship game
he threw four touchdown passes!

Most kids seemed to like the new student who moved in from out of state.

Well, except for Stewart; he didn't think Blaine Kiffen was all that great.

SCHOOL RULES

BE NICE!
BE KIND!
BE
RESPONSIBLE!

I found out later they both lived in Meadowview Apartments and rode Bus 58.

This explained why riding the bus every day was something Stewart had come to hate.

One day at lunch, it became very clear to Willie what was going on.

Blaine hung out with some of the crew while Stewart sat alone on the lawn.

7

Good ol' Stewart just wasn't acting like his normal self;
he seemed stressed and sad.
It turned out that Blaine Kiffen was calling him names
and bullying him pretty bad.

At first he tried to ignore him but that didn't help how he felt.

On the bus, Blaine kept flicking him on the ear and it left a big ol' red welt.

His daddy said,

Son, how long are you going to take that?
You need to stand up for yourself and not act scared!

But the next time Blaine bullied him, he backed down because he felt unprepared.

It got so bad that Stewart soon didn't want to go to school.
Blaine was always putting him down and treating him like a fool.

One day when Stewart was walking to class, Blaine tripped him and made him fall.

Mr. Daryl, our school custodian, saw it happen and told Blaine,

BOY, YOU HAVE SOME GALL!

But the next time it happened, Blaine knocked Stewart's books to the ground, **14** laughed, and walked on past.

Stewart thought,

Wow, I don't think this is ever going to end, Maybe I should tell an adult who can help me out.

So he put Blaine's name in the school counselor's "bully box." He could help, there was no doubt.

BULLY BOX

Mr. Jones checks the bully box every day,
so Stewart knew he would get to talk with him to see what he had to say.

Getting a piece of candy or choosing something out of the prize box in Mr. Jones' office is always fun.

But Stewart wanted to talk with him about this bully, and to his surprise, something had already been done!

Witnesses to the bullying are very important when it comes to getting this problem to cease.

They are what we call bystanders, and they are the key to bringing about peace.

19

So Mr. Jones reminded Willie and the crew that Stewart was their friend and they could help bring the continuous bullying to an end.

Here is how you

HANDLE BULLYING LIKE A B.O.S.S.

Bystanders are the deciding factor for success in a bully-free school.

They hold the key to stopping a bully and that's pretty cool.

YOU HAVE 3 CHOICES AS A BYSTANDER:

1 Join in the teasing (laughing, etc.).

2 Stand there and do nothing.

3 Help the victim!

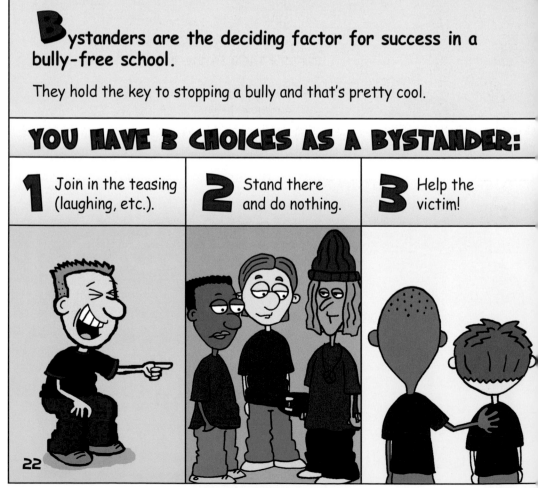

Open your mouth.

As a victim or bystander,
you can use your strong words to say,
"Hey, what are you doing?" or
"That's not cool."

Telling an adult about the bullying
is another good tool.

Stand up for others.

If you see someone being bullied and
you don't want to speak up,
just put your arm around the victim
and take them to another place.

Or tell the victim,
"Hey, I need you to come help me with something."
Just to create a little space.

Stick together. Look out for your classmates and show them some love.

You never know when you might need help
because friends stick together tighter than a glove.

23

We took his advice and now use it as our **BOEMONT "NO BULLY B.O.S.S. CREED."** It will help us overcome the harassment of bullying so we can all succeed!

So next time, don't laugh— instead stand up and say, "THAT IS JUST WRONG." Because we want everyone at our school to feel like they belong.

Another great way to show the bully that you're disapproving is to ask him the simple question, "HEY, WHAT ARE YOU DOING?"

THAT IS JUST WRONG.

HEY, WHAT ARE YOU DOING?

Willie remembered that day at lunch
when he saw Stewart was in desperate need.
He realized that he should have been following
Kendal Cobb's **"NO BULLY B.O.S.S. CREED."**

BOEMONT "NO BULLY B.O.S.S. CREED"

We are Boemont School,
we are the best.

Not being a bystander to bullying,
this is our test.

If the victim is scared
and for words they're at a loss,

Remember our Creed and handle
the Bully Like a **B.O.S.S.**

The next day in gym class, Stewart shot an air ball in the basketball game.

Then, of course, Blaine started laughing and calling him lame.

But nobody else laughed, and Willie yelled to Stewart,

Then he jumped up and blocked Blaine's shot,
knocking it into the fourth row!

After that he told him,

You're bullying my boy Stewart has got to go!

We all joke around with each other but you're crossing the line, bro!

Blaine looked shocked. He didn't think it was a big deal. Willie knew he didn't get it and it was time to keep it real.

29

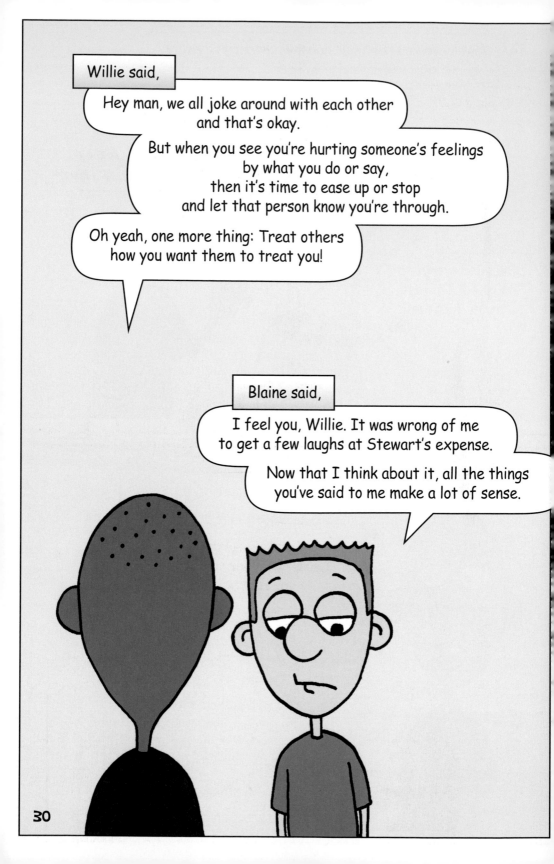

33

If **YOU** are the one being picked on, **hang in there!**

I know it can make life a pain. (Everybody deals with certain people who act like this kid named Blaine.)

If you are wondering how Blaine and Stewart are doing, there is no need to fret. Blaine has learned his lesson on how to treat other people without being such a threat.

Just know that helping out as a bystander to bullying will probably never be easy.

But maybe the Bully Song can help you; it was written by Willie's favorite rappers, Heavy B and Lil' Qeezy!

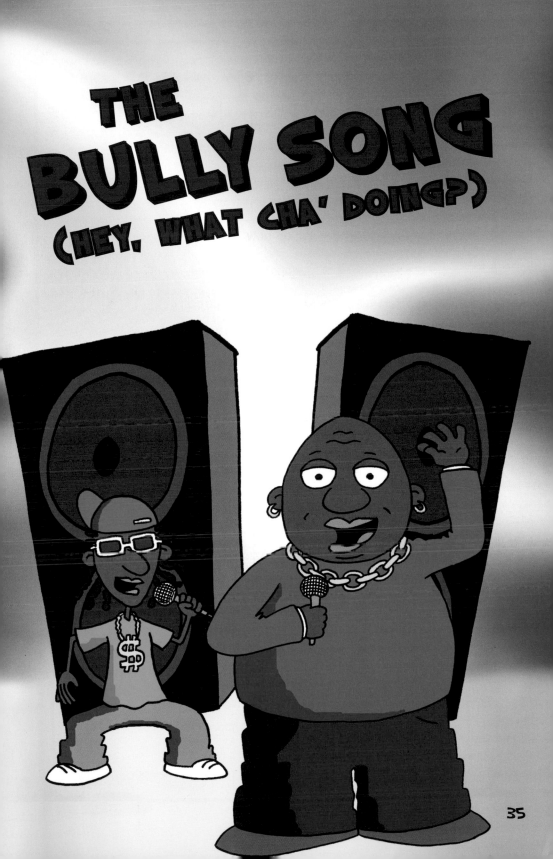

THE BULLY SONG
(HEY, WHAT CHA' DOING?)

HEY, WHAT CHA' DOING?
HEY, WHAT CHA' DOING?
HEY, WHAT CHA' DOING?
That's all you got to say!

VERSE 1
There's a bully here, you might be viewing.
A little kid that he might be chewing.
And then your mind, yeah, it starts reviewing
on what the teacher said you could be doing.
You better say it fast, and start pursuing.
Just say it now.
"HEY, WHAT CHA' DOING?"

BRIDGE
B-U-L-L-Y-I-N-G!
Why is that bully always picking on me?

VERSE 2
A bully talks big, he's looking for some fame,
he's mad at the world so he finds someone to blame
For HIS downfalls. Yeah, he makes a lot,
so he picks you out of the crowd.
Then you know what you got?
Big PROBLEMS, cause he's bigger than the rest.
So listen to your teacher, take notes for the bully test.

VERSE 3
The bully's big, yeah he's extra large.
But you were near, so you took charge.
The girl was crying, yes he made her cry.
"Hey, what cha' doing?" was your reply.
The bully stopped. He looked around.
No one's laughing, not a sound.
These things you're doing, I'm not approving.
So I ask again,
"HEY, WHAT CHA' DOING?"

WHAT IS BIBLIO-RHYMOLOGY?

Biblio-Rhymology is a proactive character-building, "ARTS"-based curriculum used in children's books to better enhance the learning style of your "right-brain" thinking students.

Biblio-Rhymology uses the 7 Building Blocks of Success

1 **DIVERSITY** – Stories include relatable characters students can connect with.

2 **RHYMES** – Stories are told in rhymes that help with reading fluency and phonological awareness.

3 **MNEMONICS** – Stories include a mnemonic that gives students a holistic image to help in retention.

4 **RAP SONGS** – Stories include a rap song that employs the emotion of music to help promote long-term memory *(see page 36)*.

5 **ART PROJECTS** – Each story includes many art projects to give the visual student something to connect with *(see Activity Guide)*.

6 **DANCE** – Every story includes a dance that opens up neurological pathways for patterns, numbers, and spatial awareness *(see Activity Guide)*.

7 **SKITS** – Each story includes a skit so students can apply the life-skill character trait in real-life situations *(see Activity Guide)*.

FOR TEACHERS

1. **Talk with your students about bullying for a few minutes every day.** Finding time for this in your busy teaching schedule might be difficult, but children must know they can talk to you anytime they see or experience bullying in any way.

2. **Make sure students know safe ways to be more than a bystander** (e.g., they can tell a teacher or another trusted adult). Helping kids learn what they can do when they see bullying can help put an end to bullying.

3. **Forty-nine states have laws that require schools to have anti-bullying policies.** Know your state's anti-bullying laws, your school's policy, and what it says about reporting bullying.

4. **Learn how to support all students when it comes to bullying.** Whether a student is a bully, a victim, or a bystander, it is important to know what steps to take and what steps to avoid in resolving a bullying situation.

5. **Take an active role in anti-bullying initiatives.** The key to addressing bullying is to stop it before it starts. Work with your students, the school, and the community to raise awareness and take action.

TIPS FOR DEALING WITH BULLYING

FOR PARENTS

Look for these signs or changes in behavior that might indicate your child is being bullied. Remember that not all children who are being bullied will exhibit warning signs.

- Lost, damaged, or destroyed clothing, books, electronics, or jewelry
- Feeling sick or faking illness (headaches, stomachaches)
- Changes in eating habits (skipping meals, binge eating, coming home hungry)
- Difficulty sleeping or frequent nightmares
- Declining grades, loss of interest in schoolwork, or not wanting to go to school
- Self-destructive behaviors such as running away from home, self-harm, or talking about suicide
- Sudden loss of friends or avoidance of social situations
- Feelings of helplessness or decreased self-esteem

How to talk with your child if you think he or she is being bullied:

- Choose an appropriate time to ask your child about suspected bullying. It might be during your drive home from school or during an after-dinner walk. Creating a space where your child is comfortable and doesn't have to look you in the eye might help him or her open up.

- Let your child do the talking.

- Listen and don't judge your child. Encourage him or her to provide as many details as possible, and document what your child tells you.

- Use open-ended questions to encourage your child to talk about what is going on at school.
    - For example: *"What did you like the most about your day?"* or *"What was the most frustrating part of your day?"*

- Don't start a conversation if you don't have time for it or know you'll be interrupted.

- If your child confirms he or she is being bullied, brainstorm how he or she can deal with the situation.
    - Encourage your child to walk away from or ignore the bully
    - If it happened at school, encourage your child to report the bullying and, if necessary, go with your child to talk to a school official.

- Praise your child for talking to you about bullying! And let your child know that being bullied is not his or her fault.

Why doesn't my child ask for help?

- Bullying can make a child feel helpless. Kids may want to try to regain control on their own. Or, they may fear being seen as weak or a tattletale if they ask for help.

- Kids may fear backlash from the bully.

- Bullying can be a humiliating experience. Kids may not want adults to know what is happening to them, or may worry that adults will judge or punish them.

- Kids who are bullied may feel socially isolated, or feel like no one cares or could understand.

- Kids may fear being rejected by or losing the support of their peers, especially friends who might be helping to protect them.

If your child is being bullied at school, you can contact a teacher, a school counselor, the principal, the superintendent, or the State Department of Education.

For more parenting information, visit boystown.org/parenting.

BOYS TOWN. Parenting

The **Boys Town National Hotline®** is open 24/7, year-round for children and adults who need help with a bullying issue. Teens also can visit the Hotline's website, YourLifeYourVoice.org, to share concerns or get immediate assistance in a crisis.

Teachers and Students! Check out Willie on Facebook and Twitter!
Willie's Twitter: @WillieBohanon | Willie's Facebook: facebook.com/williebohanon

MR. J's BULLY NOTES

1 Try to **IGNORE** the bully.

2 **DON'T** act scared.

3 Get your **STRONG WORDS** out.
The bully's hard of hearing so you may
have to shout, "**STOP! LEAVE ME ALONE!**"
and please try your best not to let
him see you pout.

4 Last but not least, **GO TELL A GROWNUP.**
They'll help keep the peace!

Look for more *Willie Bohanon Urban Character Education* series titles.
Activity Guides are available via download. Vist BoysTownPress.org.

978-1-934490-66-2   978-1-934490-73-0   978-1-934490-79-2   978-1-934490-84-6

BOYS TOWN® Press

**For information on Boys Town and its Education Model®,
Common Sense Parenting®, and training programs,** visit
boystowntraining.org or boystown.org/parenting, or contact
training@BoysTown.org or 1-800-545-5771.